KT-372-002

Leabharlanna Dhún Laoghaire · Ráth An Dúin

For Anders & Stefan, my little birds
—K.H.

In loving memory of Angeline Roy Gibson
—S.G.

Text copyright © 2015 by Kirsten Hall
Illustrations copyright © 2015 by Sabina Gibson
All rights reserved
CIP data is available.
Published in the United States 2015 by
🍎 Blue Apple Books
515 Valley Street, Maplewood, NJ 07040
www.blueapplebooks.com
Printed in China
ISBN: 978-1-60905-520-2
1 3 5 7 9 10 8 6 4 2
02/15

Little Bird,
Be Quiet!

Kirsten Hall

illustrated by
Sabina Gibson

BLUE APPLE

Little Bird loved to talk.

He talked about
the sun
and the leaves,

and the flies
and the wind,

and the fish
and the rain,

and anything
that popped into
his mind.

He tried to talk to his mother about teeth.

He tried to talk to his father about rain.

He tried to tell his sister a joke.

And he wanted to share what he learned with his brother.

Frog thought
Little Bird
was boring.

Deer
said that
Little Bird
was too loud.

And Rabbit
wished he would hurry up
and get to the point!

They all said,

"Be Quiet, Little Bird!"

Little Bird flew
until his tiny wings
could carry him no farther.

He settled beside a brook.

Another little bird looked up at him.

Little Bird wondered if this bird
would tell him to be quiet, too.

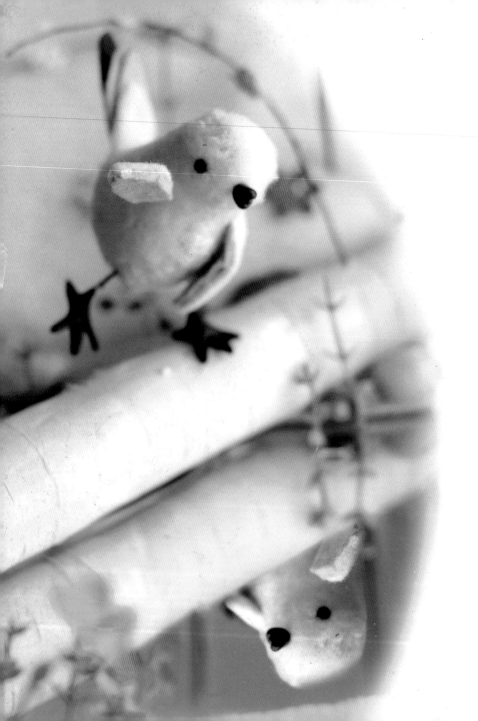

But the bird
in the water
smiled, laughed,
and flapped
his wings
at everything
Little Bird said.

Words began
to pour out
from him.

Wow! You have really small wings, just like mine!
Did you fall a lot when you were learning to fly, too?
My brother and sister flew perfectly their first times out of the nest. Amazing, right? They're older than I am, you know.
Lately they don't want me around as much. But sometimes they let me hang out with them, which is so much fun!
Last weekend we went hunting.
Oh! Let me show you something! My father taught me this really cool trick...

Back home at the breakfast table,
no one knew what to say.

It was so . . . quiet.

Out in the forest,
no one told any jokes or stories.

Something was . . .
missing.

We miss
Little
Bird.

Let's go
find him!

Little Bird
heard them coming
and flew to a high branch
in a tall tree.
He wasn't sure he
wanted to be found.

As Little Bird
listened to his friends
and family talking,

he found it almost impossible
not to call out to them.

Suddenly, Little Bird could no longer keep quiet.

47!

It takes
47 flaps—
not 46!

His mother wrapped
her warm wings around him.

Won't you
please come home,
Little Bird?

It's not the same
without you.

Little Bird was so happy.
He had so many words he wanted to say.

But for once, Little Bird just said . . .